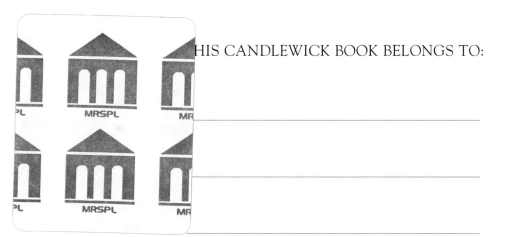

THIS CANDLEWICK BOOK BELONGS TO:

_____

_____

_____

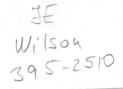
To my editor, Mary Lee Donovan, with valentines!
S. W.

To Mary Lee Donovan and Anne Moore with thanks
M. S.

Text copyright © 1999 by Sarah Wilson
Illustrations copyright © 1999 by Melissa Sweet

First paperback edition 2006

The Library of Congress has cataloged
the hardcover edition as follows:

Wilson, Sarah.
Love and kisses / Sarah Wilson;
illustrated by Melissa Sweet—1st ed.
p.   cm.
Summary: A young girl kisses her cat who kisses
a cow who kisses a goose and so on until it
comes back to where it began.
ISBN 1-56402-792-9 (hardcover)
[1. Kissing—Fiction. 2. Animals—Fiction.
3. Stories in rhyme.]
I. Sweet, Melissa, ill. II. Title.
PZ8.3.W698Lo   1999
[E]—dc21   98-23820

ISBN 0-7636-1049-6 (board book)
ISBN 0-7636-2011-4 (paperback)

2 4 6 8 10 9 7 5 3

Printed in China

This book was typeset in Lemonade.
The pictures were done in watercolor,
gouache, and collage.

Candlewick Press
2067 Massachusetts Avenue
Cambridge, Massachusetts 02140
visit us at www.candlewick.com

Love
and
Kisses

Sarah Wilson

illustrated by
Melissa Sweet

CANDLEWICK PRESS
CAMBRIDGE, MASSACHUSETTS

Blow a kiss and let it go,

You never know how love will grow—

Smooch
and smack!
You kiss your cat.

Your cat may kiss a cow.

The cow may kiss a giggling goose,

the goose, a fish—somehow!

The fish **splish! splash!** may kiss a fox.

The frog may jump to plant a kiss

upon a friendly dog.

The dog may kiss a frisky horse

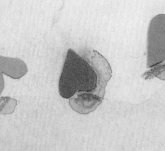

and catch him by surprise!

The horse may kiss a red-winged bird

with twinkles in her eyes.

The bird may fly to kiss a cow,

who'll laugh a great big

The cow may run to kiss a cat,

who'll then kiss . . .

you-know-who!

Kisses! Kisses!

Smooch and SMACK!

You'll have your love
and kisses back!

SARAH WILSON grew up in Maine and Massachusetts and graduated from Ohio University and the University of Madrid. She is convinced that "if there are other civilizations in other solar systems, there must be children in them." Her previous books include *Christmas Cowboy* and *Garage Song*. Sarah Wilson lives in Danville, California.

MELISSA SWEET has illustrated more than forty children's books, including the popular Pinky and Rex books by James Howe, and the acclaimed *On Christmas Day in the Morning*. She lives and works in Rockport, Maine.